ALVIN AND THE CHIPMUNKS

THE SQUEAKQUEL

BATTLE
OF THE
BANDS

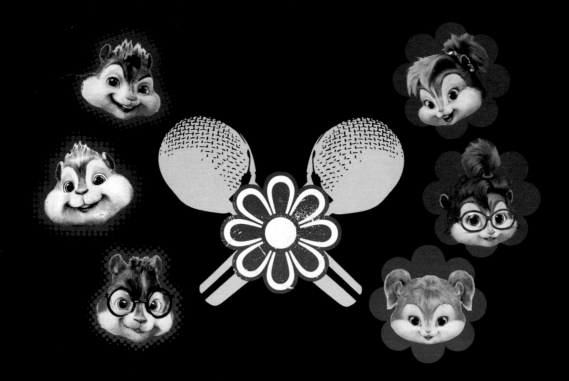

HarperFestival is an imprint of HarperCollins Publishers.
Alvin and the Chipmunks: The Squeakquel: Battle of the Bands

Library of Congress Cataloging-in-Publication Data is available.
ISBN 978-0-06-184565-9

Typography by Sean Boggs
09 10 11 12 13 UG 10 9 8 7 6 5 4 3 2 1
❖
First Edition

FOX 2000 PICTURES AND REGENCY ENTERPRISES PRESENT A BAGDASARIAN COMPANY PRODUCTION A BETTY THOMAS FILM "ALVIN AND THE CHIPMUNKS: THE SQUEAKQUEL"
ZACH LEVI DAVID CROSS AND JASON LEE AND JUSTIN LONG MATTHEW GRAY GUBLER JESSE McCARTNEY AMY POEHLER ANNA FARIS CHRISTINA APPLEGATE
COSTUME DESIGNER ALEXANDRA WELKER EXECUTIVE MUSIC PRODUCER ALI DEE THEODORE MUSIC SUPERVISOR JULIANNE JORDAN MUSIC BY DAVID NEWMAN ANIMATION SUPERVISOR CHRIS BAILEY FILM EDITOR MATTHEW FRIEDMAN
PRODUCTION DESIGNER MARCIA HINDS DIRECTOR OF PHOTOGRAPHY ANTHONY B. RICHMOND, ASC/BSC EXECUTIVE PRODUCERS KAREN ROSENFELT ARNON MILCHAN MICHELE IMPERATO STABILE STEVE WATERMAN
PRODUCED BY JANICE KARMAN ROSS BAGDASARIAN BASED UPON THE CHARACTERS "ALVIN AND THE CHIPMUNKS" CREATED BY ROSS BAGDASARIAN SCREENPLAY BY WILL McROBB AND CHRIS VISCARDI DIRECTED BY BETTY THOMAS

  www.munkyourself.com

ALVIN AND THE CHIPMUNKS™

THE SQUEAKQUEL

BATTLE OF THE BANDS

Adapted by Annie Auerbach

HARPER FESTIVAL
An Imprint of HarperCollinsPublishers

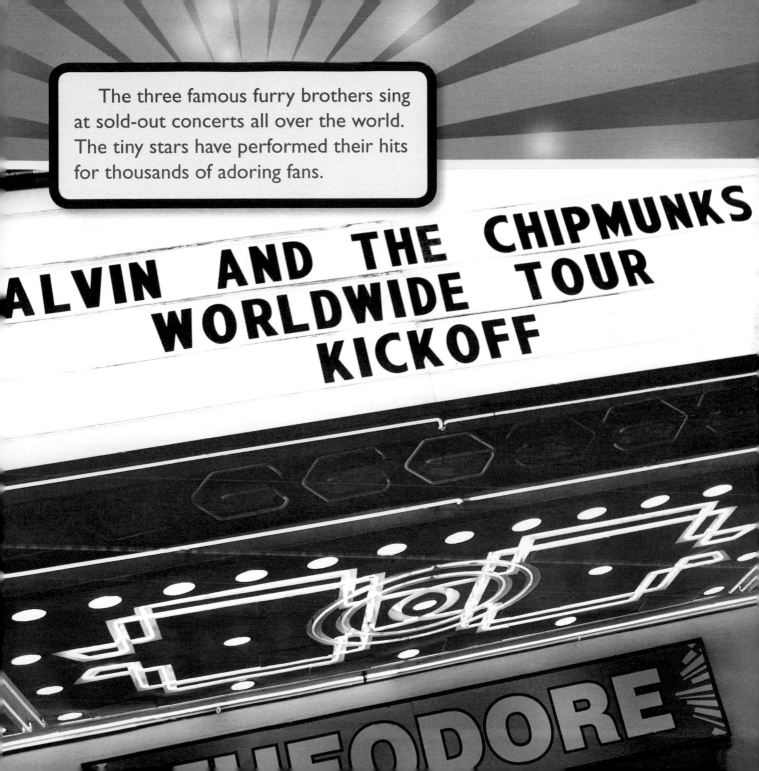

The three famous furry brothers sing at sold-out concerts all over the world. The tiny stars have performed their hits for thousands of adoring fans.

ALVIN AND THE CHIPMUNKS
WORLDWIDE TOUR
KICKOFF

THEODORE

SIMON

Favorite color: blue

Instruments: guitar, keyboards, bass, saxophone, bagpipes, tuba, drums, xylophone, glockenspiel

The Smart One

ALVIN

Favorite color: red

Instruments: lead guitar

Trouble!

THEODORE

Favorite color: green

Instruments: guitar, drums, triangle, tambourine

The Cute, Shy One

During a charity concert, Alvin got carried away. Showing off, he scampered up to the top of a tall light tower.

The tower accidentally toppled onto David Seville, The Chipmunks' adoptive father and manager. Dave had to be rushed to the hospital!

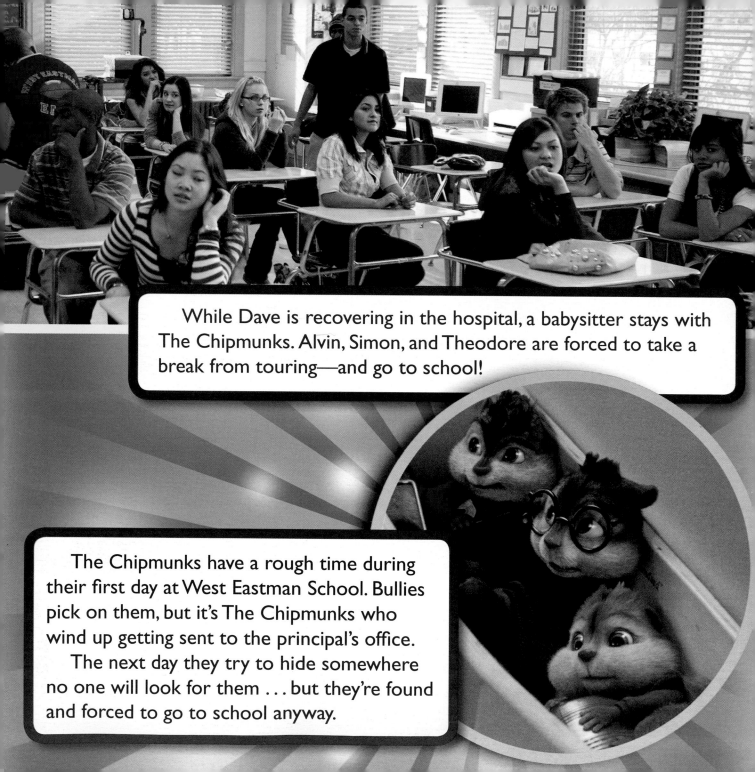

While Dave is recovering in the hospital, a babysitter stays with The Chipmunks. Alvin, Simon, and Theodore are forced to take a break from touring—and go to school!

The Chipmunks have a rough time during their first day at West Eastman School. Bullies pick on them, but it's The Chipmunks who wind up getting sent to the principal's office.

The next day they try to hide somewhere no one will look for them . . . but they're found and forced to go to school anyway.

Luckily, Principal Rubin is a huge fan of The Chipmunks. She asks them to try to save the school's music program by entering a music competition. If they win, the school will get $25,000! The Chipmunks agree to help.

At school, Alvin, Simon, and Theodore whirl around when they hear locker doors slam behind them. Standing in the hallway are three sassy *girl* chipmunks! They introduce themselves as Brittany, Jeanette, and Eleanor.

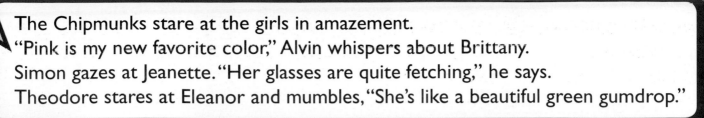

The Chipmunks stare at the girls in amazement.
"Pink is my new favorite color," Alvin whispers about Brittany.
Simon gazes at Jeanette. "Her glasses are quite fetching," he says.
Theodore stares at Eleanor and mumbles, "She's like a beautiful green gumdrop."

JEANETTE

Favorite color: blue

Quote: "We sing together or not at all."

The Absentminded Professor

BRITTANY

Favorite color: pink

Quote: "We made it, girls!"

Loves looking at herself in the mirror!

ELEANOR

Favorite color: green

Quote: "Living large!"

The Sporty One

Alvin, Simon, and Theodore soon discover that the female chipmunks are also singers in a group called The Chipettes. Their manager is Ian Hawke, The Chipmunks' old band manager! Ian is a total creep. He controlled The Chipmunks' career until they realized he was a money-hungry crook. Ian even kept The Chipmunks in a cage!

IAN HAWKE
RECORDS

Alvin tries to warn Brittany about Ian, but she doesn't want to listen. Instead, she wants to be in the music competition! Principal Rubin decides that the whole student body will watch both bands perform and vote on who's better to represent the school. It's a showdown!

The Chipettes play a song first. They're amazing, and the crowd loves them. The Chipmunks are going to have to be great to beat The Chipettes!

But Alvin has been drafted onto the school's football team for their big game. It's right before he's supposed to perform with The Chipmunks! He's sure he'll finish in time to join his brothers onstage.

The West Eastman Eagles are losing in the final quarter. It's time for a secret play called The Big A.

The quarterback hurls the football into the end zone. Alvin rides the football through the air, and lands on his feet . . . holding the ball! He scores the winning touchdown!

Nobody has ever seen a football play like The Big A— or a player like Alvin! The crowd goes wild!

Alvin is West Eastman School's new hero. The fans in the stands chant his name, as the team parades him around the stadium.

Alvin gets caught up in the excitement and forgets all about his brothers and the performance. "I'm the king of the world!" cheers Alvin.

After the celebration, Alvin rushes to the auditorium to perform ... but he's too late. His brothers wouldn't go on without him. The Chipettes won the showdown.

Theodore and Simon are seriously ticked off. The Chipettes will represent the school in the music competition.

But The Chipettes' mean manager, Ian, gets an offer for the girls to sing at a big arena. When the girls say they don't want to miss the school performance, Ian kidnaps the girls and puts them in a cage! They're going to miss the music competition!

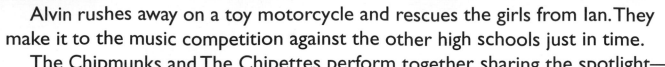

Alvin rushes away on a toy motorcycle and rescues the girls from Ian. They make it to the music competition against the other high schools just in time.

The Chipmunks and The Chipettes perform together, sharing the spotlight—and they put on an awesome show!

When they finish, the crowd gives the chipmunk supergroup a standing ovation. They win the $25,000 for the school!
Even Dave made it out of the hospital to catch the concert.

The Chipmunks give Dave a big hug. Dave agrees that The Chipettes can stay with him, too!

Alvin is so excited he bumps into a tower of sound equipment. The speakers topple on top of Dave.

"ALVIN!!!" Dave hollers.